HORRID HENRY

Francesca Simon spent her childhood on the beach in California, and then went to Yale and Oxford Universities to study medieval history and literature. She now lives in London with her family. She has written over 45 books and won the Children's Book of the Year in 2008 at the Galaxy British Book Awards for *Horrid Henry and the Abominable Snowman*.

Also by Francesca Simon

Horrid Henry
Horrid Henry Tricks the Tooth Fairy
Horrid Henry's Nits
Horrid Henry Gets Rich Quick
Horrid Henry's Haunted House
Horrid Henry and the Mummy's Curse
Horrid Henry's Revenge
Horrid Henry and the Bogey Babysitter
Horrid Henry's Stinkbomb
Horrid Henry's Underpants
Horrid Henry Meets the Queen
Horrid Henry and the Mega-Mean Time Machine
Horrid Henry and the Football Fiend
Horrid Henry's Christmas Cracker
Horrid Henry and the Abominable Snowman
Horrid Henry Robs the Bank

Horrid Henry's Big Bad Book
Horrid Henry's Wicked Ways
Horrid Henry's Evil Enemies
Horrid Henry Rules the World

Don't Cook Cinderella
Helping Hercules

and for younger readers
Don't Be Horrid, Henry

HORRID HENRY

Francesca Simon
Illustrated by Tony Ross

Orion
Children's Books

For Joshua and his friends —
Dominic, Eleanor, Freddie, Harry,
Joe, Robbie, and Toby,
with love

First published in Great Britain in 1994
by Orion Children's Books
First published in paperback in 1995
Reissued in paperback 2008
by Orion Children's Books
a division of the Orion Publishing Group Ltd
Orion House
5 Upper Saint Martin's Lane
London WC2H 9EA
An Hachette Livre UK Company

The Orion Publishing Group's policy is to use papers that are natural,
renewable and recyclable products and made from wood grown in
sustainable forests. The logging and manufacturing processes are expected to
conform to the environmental regulations of the country of origin.

A catalogue record for this book is available from the British Library.

Printed in Great Britain by Clays Ltd, St Ives plc

www.horridhenry.co.uk
www.orionbooks.co.uk

CONTENTS

1

HORRID HENRY'S PERFECT DAY

Henry was horrid.

Everyone said so, even his mother.

Henry threw food, Henry snatched, Henry pushed and shoved and pinched. Even his teddy, Mr Kill, avoided him when possible.

His parents despaired.

"What are we going to do about that horrid boy?" sighed Mum.

"How did two people as nice as us have such a horrid child?" sighed Dad.

When Horrid Henry's parents took Henry to school they walked behind him and pretended he was not theirs.

Children pointed at Henry and whispered to their parents, "That's Horrid Henry."

"He's the boy who threw my jacket in the mud."

"He's the boy who squashed Billy's beetle."

"He's the boy who . . ." Fill in whatever terrible deed you like. Horrid Henry was sure to have done it.

Horrid Henry had
a younger brother.
His name was
Perfect Peter.

Perfect Peter
always said "Please"
and "Thank you".
Perfect Peter loved
vegetables.

Perfect Peter
always used a hankie
and never, ever
picked his nose.

"Why can't you
be perfect like
Peter?" said Henry's
mum every day.

As usual, Henry pretended not to hear. He continued melting Peter's crayons on the radiator.

But Horrid Henry started to think.

"What if *I* were perfect?" thought Henry. "I wonder what would happen."

When Henry woke the next morning, he did not wake Peter by pouring water on Peter's head.

Peter did not scream.

This meant Henry's parents overslept and Henry and Peter were late for Cubs.

Henry was very happy.

Peter was very sad to be late for Cubs.

But because he was perfect, Peter did not whine or complain.

On the way to Cubs Henry did not squabble with Peter over who sat in front. He did not pinch Peter and he did not shove Peter.

Back home, when Perfect Peter built a castle, Henry did not knock it down. Instead, Henry sat on the sofa and read a book.

Mum and Dad ran into the room.

"It's awfully quiet in here," said Mum. "Are you being horrid, Henry?"

"No," said Henry.

"Peter, is Henry knocking your castle down?"

Peter longed to say "yes". But that would be a lie.

"No," said Peter.

He wondered why Henry was behaving so strangely.

"What are you doing, Henry?" said Dad.

"Reading a wonderful story about some super mice," said Henry.

Dad had never seen Henry read a book before. He checked to see if a comic was hidden inside.

There was no comic. Henry was actually reading a book.

"Hmmmm," said Dad.

It was almost time for dinner. Henry was hungry and went into the kitchen where Dad was cooking.

But instead of shouting, "I'm starving! Where's my food?" Henry said, "Dad, you look tired. Can I help get supper ready?"

"Don't be horrid, Henry," said Dad, pouring peas into boiling water. Then he stopped.

"What did you say, Henry?" asked Dad.

"Can *I* help, Dad?" said Perfect Peter.

"I asked if you needed any help," said Henry.

"I asked first," said Peter.

"Henry will just make a mess," said Dad. "Peter, would you peel the carrots while I sit down for a moment?"

"Of course," said
Perfect Peter.

Peter washed his
spotless hands.

Peter put on his
spotless apron.

Peter rolled up his
spotless sleeves.

Peter waited for
Henry to snatch the
peeler.

But Henry laid the table instead.

Mum came into the kitchen.

"Smells good," she said. "Thank you, darling Peter, for laying the table. What a good boy you are."

Peter did not say anything.

"I laid the table, Mum," said Henry.

Mum stared at him.

"You?" said Mum.

"Me," said Henry.

"Why?" said Mum.

Henry smiled.

"To be helpful," he said.

"You've done something horrid, haven't you, Henry?" said Dad.

"No," said Henry. He tried to look sweet.

"I'll lay the table tomorrow," said Perfect Peter.

"Thank you, angel," said Mum.

"Dinner is ready," said Dad.

The family sat down at the table.

Dinner was spaghetti and meatballs with peas and carrots.

Henry ate his dinner with his knife and fork and spoon.

He did not throw peas at Peter and he did not slurp.

He did not chew with his mouth open and he did not slouch.

"Sit properly, Henry," said Dad.

"I am sitting properly," said Henry.

Dad looked up from his plate. He looked surprised.

"So you are," he said.

Perfect Peter could not eat. Why wasn't Henry throwing peas at him?

Peter's hand reached slowly for a pea.

When no one was looking, he
flicked the pea at Henry.

"Ouch," said Henry.

"Don't be horrid, Henry," said
Mum.

Henry reached for a fistful of peas.
Then Henry remembered he was
being perfect and stopped.

Peter smiled and waited. But no
peas bopped him on the head.

Perfect Peter did not understand.
Where was the foot that always
kicked him under the table?

Slowly, Peter stretched out his foot and kicked Henry.

"OUCH," said Henry.

"Don't be horrid, Henry," said Dad.

"But I . . ." said Henry, then stopped.

Henry's foot wanted to kick Perfect Peter round the block. Then Henry remembered he was being perfect and continued to eat.

"You're very quiet tonight, Henry," said Dad.

"The better to enjoy my lovely dinner," said Henry.

"Henry, where are your peas and carrots?" asked Mum.

"I ate them," said Henry. "They were delicious."

Mum looked on the floor. She looked under Henry's chair. She looked under his plate.

"You ate your peas and carrots?" said Mum slowly. She felt Henry's forehead.

"Are you feeling all right, Henry?"

"Yeah," said Horrid Henry. "I'm fine, thank you for asking," he added quickly.

Mum and Dad looked at each other. What was going on?

Then they looked at Henry.

"Henry, come here and let me give you a big kiss," said Mum. "You are a wonderful boy. Would you like a piece of fudge cake?"

Peter interrupted.

"No cake for me, thank you," said Peter. "I would rather have more vegetables."

Henry let himself be kissed. Oh my, it was hard work being perfect.

He smiled sweetly at Peter.

"I would love some cake, thank you," said Henry.

Perfect Peter could stand it no longer. He picked up his plate and aimed at Henry.

Then Peter threw the spaghetti.

Henry ducked.

SPLAT!

Spaghetti landed on Mum's head. Tomato sauce trickled down her neck and down her new yellow fuzzy jumper.

"PETER!!!!" yelled Mum and Dad.

"YOU HORRID BOY!" yelled Mum.

"GO TO YOUR ROOM!!" yelled Dad.

Perfect Peter burst into tears and ran to his room.

Mum wiped spaghetti off her face. She looked very funny.

Henry tried not to laugh. He squeezed his lips together tightly.

But it was no use. I am sorry to say that he could not stop a laugh escaping.

"It's not funny!" shouted Dad.

"Go to your room!" shouted Mum.

But Henry didn't care.

Who would have thought being perfect would be such fun?

HORRID HENRY'S DANCE CLASS

Stomp Stomp Stomp Stomp Stomp Stomp Stomp.

Horrid Henry was practising his elephant dance.

Tap Tap Tap Tap Tap Tap Tap Tap.

Perfect Peter was practising his raindrop dance.

Peter was practising being a raindrop for his dance class show.

Henry was also supposed to be practising being a raindrop.

But Henry did not want to be a raindrop. He did not want to be a tomato, a string bean, or a banana either.

Stomp Stomp Stomp went Henry's heavy boots.

Tap Tap Tap went Peter's tap shoes.

"You're doing it wrong, Henry," said Peter.

"No I'm not," said Henry.

"You are too," said Peter. "We're supposed to be raindrops."

Stomp Stomp Stomp went Henry's boots. He was an elephant smashing his way through the jungle, trampling on everyone who stood in his way.

"I can't concentrate with you stomping," said Peter. "And I have to practise my solo."

"Who cares?" screamed Horrid Henry. "I hate dancing, I hate dance class, and most of all, I hate you!"

This was not entirely true. Horrid Henry loved dancing. Henry danced in his bedroom. Henry danced up and down the stairs. Henry danced on the new sofa and on the kitchen table.

What Henry hated was having to dance with other children.

"Couldn't I go to karate instead?" asked Henry every Saturday.

"No," said Mum. "Too violent."

"Judo?" said Henry.

"N–O spells no," said Dad.

So every Saturday morning at 9.45
a.m., Henry and Peter's father drove
them to Miss Impatience Tutu's
Dance Studio.

Miss Impatience Tutu was skinny and bony. She had long stringy grey hair. Her nose was sharp. Her elbows were pointy. Her knees were knobbly. No one had ever seen her smile.

Perhaps this was because Impatience Tutu hated teaching.

Impatience Tutu hated noise.

Impatience Tutu hated children.

But most of all Impatience Tutu hated Horrid Henry.

This was not surprising. When Miss

Tutu shouted, "Class, lift your left legs," eleven left legs lifted. One right leg sagged to the floor.

When Miss Tutu screamed, "Heel, toe, heel, toe," eleven dainty feet tapped away. One clumpy foot stomped toe, heel, toe, heel.

When Miss Tutu bellowed, "Class, skip to your right," eleven bodies turned to the right. One body galumphed to the left.

Naturally, no one wanted to dance with Henry. Or indeed, anywhere near Henry. Today's class, unfortunately, was no different.

"Miss Tutu, Henry is treading on my toes," said Jumpy Jeffrey.

"Miss Tutu, Henry is kicking my legs," said Lazy Linda.

"Miss Tutu, Henry is bumping me," said Vain Violet.

"HENRY!" screeched Miss Tutu.

"Yeah," said Henry.

"I am a patient woman, and you are trying my patience to the limit," hissed Miss Tutu. "Any more bad behaviour and you will be very sorry."

"What will happen?" asked Horrid Henry eagerly.

Miss Tutu stood very tall. She took a long, bony finger and dragged it slowly across her throat.

Henry decided that he would rather live to do battle another day. He stood on the side, gnashing his teeth, pretending he was an enormous crocodile about to gobble up Miss Tutu.

"This is our final rehearsal before the show," barked Miss Tutu. "Everything must be perfect."

Eleven faces stared at Miss Tutu. One face scowled at the floor.

"Tomatoes and beans to the front," ordered Miss Tutu.

"When Miss Thumper plays the music everyone will stretch out their arms to the sky, to kiss the morning hello. Raindrops, stand at the back next to the giant green leaves and wait until the beans find the magic bananas. And Henry," spat Miss Tutu, glaring. "TRY to get it right.

"Positions, everybody. Miss Thumper, the opening music please!" shouted Miss Tutu.

Miss Thumper banged away.

The tomatoes weaved in and out, twirling.

The beans pirouetted.

The bananas pointed their toes and swayed.

The raindrops pitter-patted.

All except one. Henry waved his arms frantically and raced round the room. Then he crashed into the beans.

"HENRY!" screeched Miss Tutu.

"Yeah," scowled Henry.

"Sit in the corner!"

Henry was delighted. He sat in the corner and made horrible rude faces while Peter did his raindrop solo.

Tap tap tap tap tap tap tap. Tappa tappa tappa tappa tap tap tap. Tappa tip tappa tip tappa tappa tappa tip.

"Was that perfect, Miss Tutu?" asked Peter.

Miss Tutu sighed. "Perfect, Peter, as always," she said, and the corner of her mouth trembled slightly. This was the closest Miss Tutu ever came to smiling.

Then she saw Henry slouching on

the chair. Her mouth drooped back into its normal grim position.

Miss Tutu tugged Henry off the chair. She shoved him to the very back of the stage, behind the other raindrops. Then she pushed him behind a giant green leaf.

"Stand there!" shouted Miss Tutu.

"But no one will see me here," said Henry.

"Precisely," said Miss Tutu.

It was showtime.

The curtain was about to rise.

The children stood quietly on stage.

Perfect Peter was so excited he almost bounced up and down. Naturally he controlled himself and stood still.

Horrid Henry was not very excited.

He did not want to be a raindrop.

And he certainly did not want to be a raindrop who danced behind a giant green leaf.

Miss Thumper waddled over to the piano. She banged on the keys.

The curtain went up.

Henry's mum and dad were in the audience with the other parents. As usual they sat in the back row, in case they had to make a quick getaway.

They smiled and waved at Peter, standing proudly at the front.

"Can you see Henry?" whispered Henry's mum.

Henry's dad squinted at the stage.

A tuft of red hair stuck up behind the green leaf.

"I think that's him behind the leaf," said his father doubtfully.

"I wonder why Henry is hiding," said Mum. "It's not like him to be shy."

"Hmmmm," said Dad.

"Shhh," hissed the parents beside them.

Henry watched the tomatoes and beans searching on tiptoe for the magic bananas.

I'm not staying back here, he thought, and pushed his way through the raindrops.

"Stop pushing, Henry!" hissed Lazy Linda.

Henry pushed harder, then did a few pitter-pats with the other raindrops.

Miss Tutu stretched out a bony arm and yanked Henry back behind the scenery.

Who wants to be a raindrop anyway, thought Henry. I can do what I like hidden here.

The tomatoes weaved in and out, twirling.

The beans pirouetted.

The bananas pointed their toes and swayed.

The raindrops pitter-patted.

Henry flapped his arms and pretended he was a *pterodactyl* about to pounce on Miss Tutu.

Round and round he flew, homing in on his prey.

Perfect Peter stepped to the front and began his solo.

Tap Tap Tap Tap Tap Tap –
CRASH!

One giant green leaf fell on top of
the raindrops, knocking them over.

The raindrops collided with the
tomatoes.

The tomatoes smashed into the
string beans.

The string beans bumped into the
bananas.

Perfect Peter turned his head to see
what was happening and danced off
the stage into the front row.

Miss Tutu fainted.

The only person
still standing on
stage was Henry.

Stomp Stomp
Stomp Stomp
Stomp Stomp
Stomp.

Henry did his
elephant dance.
Boom Boom
Boom Boom Boom
Boom Boom.
Henry did his
wild buffalo dance.

Peter tried to scramble back on stage.

The curtain fell.

There was a long silence, then Henry's parents clapped.

No one else did, so Henry's parents stopped.

All the other parents ran up to Miss Tutu and started shouting.

"I don't see why that horrid boy should have had such a long solo while all Linda did was lie on the floor," yelled one mother.

"My Jeffrey is a much better dancer than that boy," shouted another. "He should have done the solo."

"I didn't know you taught modern dance, Miss Tutu," said Violet's mother. "Come, Violet," she added, sweeping from the room.

"HENRY!!" screeched Miss Tutu. "Leave my dance studio at once!"

"Whoopee!" shouted Henry. He knew that next Saturday he would be at karate class at last.

3

HORRID HENRY
AND
MOODY MARGARET

"I'm Captain Hook!"

"No, I'm Captain Hook!"

"I'm Captain Hook," said Horrid Henry.

"I'm Captain Hook," said Moody Margaret.

They glared at each other.

"It's *my* hook," said Moody Margaret.

Moody Margaret lived next door.

She did not like Horrid
Henry, and Horrid
Henry did not like
her. But when Rude
Ralph was busy, Clever
Clare had flu, and Sour
Susan was her enemy,
Margaret would jump
over the wall to play
with Henry.

"Actually, it's my turn to be Hook
now," said Perfect Peter. "I've been
the prisoner for such a long time."

"Prisoner, be quiet!" said Henry.

"Prisoner, walk the plank!" said
Margaret.

"But I've walked it fourteen times
already," said Peter. "Please can I be
Hook now?"

"No, by thunder!" said Moody
Margaret. "Now out of my way,

worm!" And she swashbuckled across
the deck, waving her hook and
clutching her sword and dagger.

Margaret had eyepatches and skulls
and crossbones and plumed hats and
cutlasses and sabres and snickersnees.

Henry had a stick.

This was why Henry played with
Margaret.

But Henry had to do terrible things
before playing with Margaret's

swords. Sometimes he had to sit and wait while she read a book. Sometimes he had to play "Mums and Dads" with her. Worst of all (please don't tell anyone), sometimes he had to be the baby.

Henry never knew what Margaret would do.

When he put a spider on her arm, Margaret laughed.

When he pulled her hair, Margaret pulled his harder.

When Henry screamed, Margaret would scream louder. Or she would sing. Or pretend not to hear.

Sometimes Margaret was fun. But most of the time she was a moody old grouch.

"I won't play if I can't be Hook," said Horrid Henry.

Margaret thought for a moment.

"We can both be Captain Hook," she said.

"But we only have one hook," said Henry.

"Which I haven't played with yet," said Peter.

"BE QUIET, prisoner!" shouted Margaret. "Mr Smee, take him to jail."

"No," said Henry.

"You will get your reward, Mr Smee," said the Captain, waving her hook.

Mr Smee dragged the prisoner to the jail.

"If you're very quiet, prisoner, then you will be freed and you can be a pirate, too," said Captain Hook.

"Now give me the hook," said Mr Smee.

The Captain reluctantly handed it over.

"Now I'm Captain Hook and you're Mr Smee," shouted Henry. "I order everyone to walk the plank!"

"I'm sick of playing pirates," said Margaret. "Let's play something else."

Henry was furious. That was just like Moody Margaret.

"Well, I'm playing pirates," said
Henry.

"Well I'm not," said Margaret.
"Give me back my hook."

"No," said Henry.
Moody Margaret
opened her mouth
and screamed. Once
Margaret started
screaming she could
go on and on and
on.

Henry gave her
the hook.

Margaret smiled.

"I'm hungry,"
she said. "Got
anything good to
eat?"

Henry had three bags of crisps and
seven chocolate biscuits hidden in his

room, but he certainly wasn't going to share them with Margaret.

'You can have a radish," said Henry.

"What else?" said Margaret.

"A carrot," said Henry.

"What else?" said Margaret.

"Glop," said Henry.

"What's Glop?"

"Something special that only I can make," said Henry.

"What's in it? asked Margaret.

"That's a secret," said Henry.

"I bet it's yucky," said Margaret.

"Of course it's yucky," said Henry.

"I can make the yuckiest Glop of all," said Margaret.

"That's because you don't know anything. No one can make yuckier Glop than I can."

"I dare you to eat Glop," said Margaret.

"I double dare you back," said Henry. "Dares go first."

Margaret stood up very straight.

"All right," said Margaret. "Glop starts with snails and worms."

And she started poking under the bushes.

"Got one!" she shouted, holding up a fat snail.

"Now for some worms," said Margaret.

She got down on her hands and knees and started digging a hole.

"You can't put anything from outside into Glop," said Henry quickly. "Only stuff in the kitchen."

Margaret looked at Henry.

"I thought we were making Glop," she said.

"We are," said Henry. "My way, because it's *my* house."

Horrid Henry and Moody Margaret went into the gleaming white kitchen. Henry got out two wooden mixing spoons and a giant red bowl.

"I'll start," said Henry. He went to the cupboard and opened the doors wide.

"Porridge!" said Henry. And he poured some into the bowl.

Margaret opened the fridge and

looked inside. She grabbed a small container.

"Soggy semolina!" shouted Margaret. Into the bowl it went.

"Coleslaw!"

"Spinach!"

"Coffee!"

"Yoghurt!"

"Flour!"

"Vinegar!"

"Baked beans!"

"Mustard!"

"Peanut butter!"

"Mouldy cheese!"

"Pepper!"

"Rotten oranges!"

"And ketchup!" shouted Henry. He squirted in the ketchup until the bottle was empty.

"Now, mix!" said Margaret.

Horrid Henry and Moody Margaret grabbed hold of their spoons with both hands. Then they plunged the spoons into the Glop and began to stir.

It was hard heavy work.

Faster and faster, harder and harder they stirred.

There was Glop on the ceiling. There was Glop on the floor. There was Glop on the clock, and Glop on the door. Margaret's hair was covered in Glop. So was Henry's face.

Margaret looked into the bowl. She had never seen anything so yucky in her life.

"It's ready," she said.

Horrid Henry and Moody Margaret carried the Glop to the table.

Then they sat down and stared at the sloppy, slimy, sludgy, sticky, smelly, gooey, gluey, gummy, greasy, gloopy Glop.

"Right," said Henry. "Who's going to eat some first?"

There was a very long pause.

Henry looked at Margaret.

Margaret looked at Henry.

"Me," said Margaret. "I'm not scared."

She scooped up a large spoonful and stuffed it in her mouth.

Then she
swallowed. Her face
went pink and
purple and green.

"How does it
taste?" said Henry.

"Good," said
Margaret, trying not
to choke.

"Have some more
then," said Henry.

"Your turn first,"
said Margaret.

Henry sat for a moment and looked at the Glop.

"My mum doesn't like me to eat between meals," said Henry.

"HENRY!" hissed Moody Margaret.

Henry took a tiny spoonful.

"More!" said Margaret.

Henry took a tiny bit more. The Glop wobbled lumpily on his spoon. It looked like . . . Henry did not want to think about what it looked like.

He closed his eyes and brought the spoon to his mouth.

"Ummm, yummm," said Henry.

"You didn't eat any," said Margaret. "That's not fair."

She scooped up some Glop and . . .

I dread to think what would have

happened next, if they had not been interrupted.

"Can I come out now?" called a small voice from outside. "It's my turn to be Hook."

Horrid Henry had forgotten all about Perfect Peter.

"OK," shouted Henry.

Peter came to the door.

"I'm hungry," he said.

"Come in, Peter," said Henry sweetly. "Your dinner is on the table."

HORRID HENRY'S HOLIDAY

Horrid Henry hated holidays.

Henry's idea of a super holiday was sitting on the sofa eating crisps and watching TV.

Unfortunately, his parents usually had other plans.

Once they took him to see some castles. But there were no castles. There were only piles of stones and broken walls.

"Never again," said Henry.

The next year he had to go to a lot of museums.

"Never again," said Mum and
Dad.

Last year they went to the seaside.

"The sun is too hot," Henry
whined.

"The water is too cold," Henry
whinged.

"The food is yucky," Henry grumbled.

"The bed is lumpy," Henry moaned.

This year they decided to try something different.

"We're going camping in France," said Henry's parents.

"Horray!" said Henry.

"You're happy, Henry?" said Mum. Henry had never been happy about any holiday plans before.

"Oh yes," said Henry. Finally, finally, they were doing something good.

Henry knew all about camping from Moody Margaret. Margaret had been camping with her family. They had stayed in a big tent with comfy beds, a fridge, a cooker, a loo, a shower, a heated swimming pool, a disco, and a great big giant TV with fifty-seven channels.

"Oh boy!" said Horrid Henry.

"Bonjour!" said Perfect Peter.

The great day arrived at last. Horrid Henry, Perfect Peter, Mum and Dad boarded the ferry for France.

Henry and Peter had never been on a boat before.

Henry jumped on and off the seats.

Peter did a lovely drawing.

The boat went up and down and up and down.

Henry ran back
and forth between
the aisles.

Peter pasted
stickers in his
notebook.

The boat went up
and down and up
and down.

Henry sat on a
revolving chair and
spun round.

Peter played with
his puppets.

The boat went up
and down and up
and down.

Then Henry and
Peter ate a big
greasy lunch of
sausages and chips

in the café.

The boat went up
and down, and up
and down, and up
and down.

Henry began to
feel queasy.

Peter began to
feel queasy.

Henry's face went
green.

Peter's face went
green.

"I think I'm going to be sick," said
Henry, and threw up all over Mum.

"I think I'm going to be –" said
Peter, and threw up all over Dad.

"Oh no," said Mum.

"Never mind," said Dad. "I just
know this will be our best holiday
ever."

Finally, the boat arrived in France.

After driving and driving and driving they reached the campsite.

It was even better than Henry's dreams. The tents were as big as houses. Henry heard the happy sound of TVs blaring, music playing, and children splashing and shrieking. The sun shone. The sky was blue.

"Wow, this looks great," said Henry.

But the car drove on.

"Stop!" said Henry. "You've gone too far."

"We're not staying in that awful place," said Dad.

They drove on.

"Here's our campsite,' said Dad. "A *real* campsite!"

Henry stared at the bare rocky ground under the cloudy grey sky.

There were three small tents flapping in the wind. There was a single tap. There were a few trees. There was nothing else.

"It's wonderful!" said Mum.

"It's wonderful!" said Peter.

"But where's the TV?" said Henry.

"No TV here, thank goodness," said Mum. "We've got books."

"But where are the beds?" said
Henry.

"No beds here, thank goodness,"
said Dad. "We've got sleeping bags."

"But where's the pool?" said
Henry.

"No pool," said Dad. "*We'll* swim
in the river."

"Where's the toilet?" said Peter.
Dad pointed at a distant cubicle.
Three people stood waiting.

"All the way over there?" said Peter. "I'm not complaining," he added quickly.

Mum and Dad unpacked the car. Henry stood and scowled.

"Who wants to help put up the tent?" asked Mum.

"I do!" said Dad.

"I do!" said Peter.

Henry was horrified. "We have to put up our own tent?"

"Of course," said Mum.

"I don't like it here," said Henry.

"I want to go camping in the other place."

"That's not camping," said Dad. "Those tents have beds in them. And loos. And showers. And fridges. And cookers, and TVs. Horrible." Dad shuddered.

"Horrible," said Peter.

"And we have such a lovely snug tent here," said Mum. "Nothing modern – just wooden pegs and poles."

"Well, I want to stay there," said Henry.

"We're staying here," said Dad.

"NO!" screamed Henry.

"YES!" screamed Dad.

I am sorry to say that Henry then had the longest, loudest, noisiest, shrillest, most horrible tantrum you can imagine.

Did you think that a horrid boy like Henry would like nothing better

than sleeping on
hard rocky ground
in a soggy sleeping
bag without a
pillow?

You thought
wrong.

Henry liked
comfy beds.

Henry liked crisp
sheets.

Henry liked hot
baths.

Henry liked
microwave dinners,
TV, and noise.

He did not like cold showers, fresh
air, and quiet.

Far off in the distance the sweet
sound of loud music drifted towards
them.

"Aren't you glad we're not staying in that awful noisy place?" said Dad.

"Oh yes," said Mum.

"Oh yes," said Perfect Peter.

Henry pretended he was a bulldozer come to knock down tents and squash campers.

"Henry, don't barge the tent!" yelled Dad.

Henry pretended he was a hungry *Tyrannosaurus Rex*.

"OW!" shrieked Peter.

"Henry, don't be horrid!" yelled Mum.

She looked up at the dark cloudy sky.

"It's going to rain," said Mum.

"Don't worry," said Dad. "It never rains when I'm camping."

"The boys and I will go and collect some more firewood," said Mum.

"I'm not moving," said Horrid Henry.

While Dad made a campfire, Henry played his boom-box as loud as he could, stomping in time to the terrible music of the Killer Boy Rats.

"Henry, turn that noise down this minute," said Dad.

Henry pretended not to hear.

"HENRY!" yelled Dad. "TURN THAT DOWN!"

Henry turned the volume down the teeniest tiniest fraction.

The terrible sounds of the Killer Boy Rats continued to boom over the quiet campsite.

Campers emerged from their tents and shook their fists. Dad switched off Henry's tape player.

"Anything wrong, Dad?" asked Henry, in his sweetest voice.

"No," said Dad.

Mum and Peter returned carrying armfuls of firewood.

It started to drizzle.

"This is fun," said Mum, slapping a mosquito.

"Isn't it?" said Dad. He was heating up some tins of baked beans.

The drizzle turned into a downpour.

The wind blew.

The campfire hissed, and went out.

"Never mind," said Dad brightly. "We'll eat our baked beans cold."

Mum was snoring.

Dad was snoring.

Peter was snoring.

Henry tossed and turned. But whichever way he turned in his damp sleeping bag, he seemed to be lying on sharp, pointy stones.

Above him, mosquitoes whined.

I'll never get to sleep, he thought, kicking Peter.

How am I going to bear this for fourteen days?

Around four o'clock on Day Five the family huddled inside the cold, damp, smelly tent listening to the howling wind and the pouring rain.

"Time for a walk!" said Dad.

"Great idea!" said Mum, sneezing. "I'll get the boots."

"Great idea!" said Peter, sneezing. "I'll get the macs."

"But it's pouring outside," said Henry.

"So?" said Dad. "What better time to go for a walk?"

"I'm not coming," said Horrid Henry.

"I am," said Perfect Peter. "I don't mind the rain."

Dad poked his head outside the tent.

"The rain has stopped," he said. "I'll remake the fire."

"I'm not coming," said Henry.

"We need more firewood," said Dad. "Henry can stay here and collect some. And make sure it's dry."

Henry poked his head outside the tent. The rain had stopped, but the sky was still cloudy. The fire spat.

I won't go, thought Henry. The forest will be all muddy and wet.

He looked round to see if there was any wood closer to home.

That was when he saw the thick, dry wooden pegs holding up all the tents.

Henry looked to the left.
Henry looked to the right.
No one was around.

If I just take a few pegs from each
tent, he thought, they'll never be
missed.

When Mum and Dad came back
they were delighted.

"What a lovely roaring fire," said
Mum.

"Clever you to find some dry
wood," said Dad.

The wind blew.

Henry dreamed he was floating in a cold river, floating, floating, floating.

He woke up. He shook his head. He *was* floating. The tent was filled with cold muddy water.

Then the tent collapsed on top of them.

Henry, Peter, Mum and Dad stood outside in the rain and stared at the river of water gushing through their collapsed tent.

All round them soaking wet campers were staring at their collapsed tents.

Peter sneezed.

Mum sneezed.

Dad sneezed.

Henry coughed, choked, spluttered and sneezed.

"I don't understand it," said Dad. "This tent *never* collapses."

"What are we going to do?" said Mum.

"I know," said Henry. "I've got a very good idea."

Two hours later Mum, Dad, Henry and Peter were sitting on a sofa-bed inside a tent as big as a house, eating crisps and watching TV.

The sun was shining. The sky was blue.

"Now this is what I call a holiday!" said Henry.